THE GREAT MOUSE DETECTIVE

· BOOK 7 ·

Basil and the Royal Dare

CREATED BY *Eve Titus* WRITTEN BY *Cathy Hapka*

ILLUSTRATED BY *David Mottram*

ALADDIN

NEW YORK LONDON TORONTO SYDNEY NEW DELHI

ALADDIN

An imprint of Simon & Schuster Children's Publishing Division
1230 Avenue of the Americas, New York, New York 10020
First Aladdin paperback edition May 2019
Text copyright © 2019 by Estate of Eve Titus
Illustrations copyright © 2019 by David Mottram
Also available in an Aladdin hardcover edition.
All rights reserved, including the right of reproduction in whole or in part in any form.
ALADDIN and related logo are registered trademarks of Simon & Schuster, Inc.
For information about special discounts for bulk purchases, please contact
Simon & Schuster Special Sales at 1-866-506-1949 or business@simonandschuster.com.
The Simon & Schuster Speakers Bureau can bring authors to your live event.
For more information or to book an event contact the Simon & Schuster Speakers Bureau
at 1-866-248-3049 or visit our website at www.simonspeakers.com.
Cover designed by Karin Paprocki
Interior designed by Hilary Zarycky
The text of this book was set in Perpetua.
Manufactured in the United States of America 0419 OFF
2 4 6 8 10 9 7 5 3 1
Library of Congress Control Number 2019931783
ISBN 978-1-5344-1863-9 (hc)
ISBN 978-1-5344-1862-2 (pbk)
ISBN 978-1-5344-1864-6 (eBook)

Cast of Characters

BASIL	*English mouse detective*
DR. DAWSON	*his friend and associate*
ELWOOD	*mouse messenger*
MISS HAZEL	*proprietress of Holmestead Cheese Emporium*
CECIL	*royally lazy cat*
PES	*a scoundrel of a Bohemian dog*
THE DUKE	*British mouse royal*
THE DUCHESS	*British mouse royal*
THE KING OF BOHEMIA	*royal mouse visitor*
THE QUEEN OF BOHEMIA	*royal mouse visitor*
LADISLAV	*Bohemian royal cousin*
GEORGE	*British mouse earl*
PRINCE LEO	*human Bohemian royal*
MAREK	*crown prince of Bohemia (a mouse)*
PAVLA, SILVIE, AND RADIM	*other young Bohemian royals*
CLARA	*teen daughter of the duke and duchess*
FLORRIE AND HUGO	*other young British mouse royals*
EDWARD, PRINCE OF WALES	*human royal*
PRINCESS ALEXANDRA OF DENMARK	*Edward's wife*
PRINCESS HELENA	*Edward's sister*

VARIOUS SERVANTS (MOUSE AND HUMAN), ROYAL FAMILY MEMBERS, AND OTHERS

Contents

1

AT LOOSE ENDS

"HAVE A TASTE OF THIS, BASIL." I HELD OUT A CRUMB of cheddar.

There was no response from across the table. My dear friend Basil—better known throughout mousedom as Basil of Baker Street, the world-famous detective—sat staring glumly out the front window of the Holmestead Cheese Emporium. His chin rested on his paw, his whiskers drooped, and even his deerstalker cap appeared less jaunty than usual.

I sighed. "Basil!" I said in a louder tone. "Breakfast is the most important meal of the day. Mr. Holmes says so quite frequently himself, remember? You need to eat something."

I figured that would induce Basil to eat if anything could. He admired Mr. Sherlock Holmes, the famous human detective, to no end. For some years, he had regularly dragged me through the dangerous London streets to visit the great man's study at 221B Baker Street so he could listen to Holmes's conversations with his friend Dr. John H. Watson. The two of us would hide in the walls or beneath the furniture as they discussed how Mr. Holmes solved his many cases. Eventually

Basil had struck upon the idea to build the town of Holmestead in Mr. Holmes's cellar, and there we and many other mice had lived happily since the year 1885. The cellar was warm and dry and safe from cats and other dangers, which was important to most of us. But even more important to Basil was its proximity to that study. Now we made the trip upstairs daily—sometimes more than once!

But on this particular day, Mr. Holmes was absent from the house and, in fact, from London itself. He'd departed for the Continent the previous afternoon, leaving Basil at loose ends with no case of his own to distract him from his idol's absence.

"What shall we do today, Dawson?" Basil asked me with a sigh, poking at the uneaten cheese on his plate. "Shall we take a long ramble by the Thames or pay a visit to the British Museum? Or perhaps we should stay here and assist Mrs. Judson with the laundry for want of loftier occupations."

Despite my concern for Basil's mood, I couldn't help smiling at the thought of him assisting our mousekeeper with her work. I had little doubt that my friend could conquer the laundry of all of Holmestead if he put his mind to it. But I suspected his perfectionist nature might drive poor Mrs. Judson crazy in the meantime!

"We haven't visited the museum for some time," I said. "I have no patients to see today, though I'd hoped to catch up on my paperwork."

Basil eyed me blankly. Sometimes I think he forgets entirely that I am a medical mouse—Dr. David Q. Dawson, to be precise—and not merely the sidekick for his detecting adventures!

"More cheese, sirs?" asked Miss Hazel, the proprietress of the cheese shop. "Oh dear, Mr. Basil, you haven't touched your Camembert! Is there something wrong with it?"

"Not a thing, my dear," Basil responded in his gallant way. "It is my appetite that is amiss."

Miss Hazel looked concerned. But before she could say anything else, the shop door flew open. A mouse stood there, though not one I'd ever seen before. He was nearly as tall as Basil, with an elegant set to his ears, and dressed rather formally in a cutaway coat and dark breeches.

"Pardon me," the stranger said, sweeping into a bow. "I am in search of a certain Basil of Baker

Street, the famous detective—it's rather urgent that I find him at once."

Miss Hazel and I were so startled by the well-dressed mouse's sudden appearance that we could not respond for a moment. Basil, however, is rarely at a loss for words. He stood immediately and returned the stranger's bow.

"I am the mouse you seek," he said. "How may I be of service?"

"Oh, thank goodness I've found you." The

stranger hurried forward. "I must beg of you to come with me at once. Your services are required by the noblemice of Marlborough House."

"Marlborough House?" Hazel cried. "Why, that's where the royal family lives!"

"Precisely." The stranger didn't spare her—or me—so much as a glance, keeping his gaze intent upon Basil. "Please, sir. You must come quickly!"

2

MARLBOROUGH HOUSE

"COME, DAWSON." BASIL GRABBED THE LAST BIT OF cheddar from my plate and tossed it into his mouth. "You heard the mouse. Lead the way, good sir."

The stranger did so, scurrying ahead of us out of the shop and down the street toward the basement window. Along the way, he told us that his name was Elwood.

"I work for the noblemice," he explained. "The duke sent me as a messenger to fetch you, as I am the fastest of foot."

"We shall try to keep up," Basil assured him. "Now, tell us what is wrong if you can."

I was impressed by his calmness. As for myself,

I was in awe at the thought of meeting the duke!

Elwood glanced around. Holmestead was quiet at that hour of the morning, but a few mice were out and about—shopkeepers opening their businesses, mousewives shaking out their dishrags, and others out for an early stroll. Still, Elwood shook his head.

"The noblemice prefer strict discretion when it comes to their family affairs," he said. "Therefore, I'd rather let the duke tell you why he requires your services. However, I can fill you in on some of the background."

"All right," Basil said, hopping up onto the windowsill where we would make our exit from the house. "Please begin."

Elwood nodded, following Basil through the crack in the window. I was at his heels, listening carefully to whatever he might be about to say, for I was curious. What would the noblemice of the famous Marlborough House need with Basil's detective services?

Outside, we had to remain silent for a moment as we rushed across the open street and into the relative safety of an alley. I kept a wary eye out for

cats, crows, and dogs, along with the many other dangers a mouse might face on the busy city streets.

And then a stroke of luck. Basil spotted a carriage heading south—exactly the direction we needed to go. Quick as a wink, the three of us had scampered up the wheel into the luggage rack at the back.

That gave us a chance to rest—and to hear what Elwood had to tell us.

"As you know," he began, "Marlborough House is the primary residence of the human Prince of

Wales, along with his wife and various children and other family members."

"Yes, of course," Basil said. "It is also the residence of the Duke of British Mousedom and his fine family."

I scratched my whiskers. "Hang on," I said, having only the vaguest notion of the comings and goings of the royals, mouse and human alike. "What about the king and queen? The mouse royals, that is."

"Don't be foolish, Dawson," Basil said rather sharply. "They reside at Windsor Castle with Her Majesty, Queen Victoria, of course."

"Oh, yes, of course." Feeling properly chastised, I listened in silence as Elwood continued.

"At the moment," he said, "the human royals are hosting the visiting royal family of Bohemia. The Bohemian mouse royals managed to stow along on the voyage, and the duke and duchess have been thrilled to entertain them during the visit."

"How lovely," I said politely.

Meanwhile, Basil seemed barely to have heard the last part of Elwood's speech. He was peering out at the street.

"Hurry," he said. "We're nearly to Piccadilly Circus, and I can tell by the tilt of the horse's ears that we're about to turn east toward Covent Garden."

Elwood nodded. "We'll proceed on foot from here. It's only a short journey now."

I leaped down from the carriage after them. However, I soon found fault with Elwood's proclamation. The journey certainly didn't feel short! We had to scurry all the way around Piccadilly Circus to avoid the congestion within the busy

interchange. Then it was down several other bustling streets, past Trafalgar Square, and finally down Pall Mall.

It was with relief that I spotted the stately facade of Marlborough House rising out of its well-tended grounds. "This way," Elwood instructed, darting through the fence and around the side of the massive house. As we crept along, the sound of loud, eager barking came from somewhere nearby.

"Those dogs sound big," I said nervously, glancing over my shoulder for any sign of a bounding beast heading our way.

"Those are the prince's dogs," Elwood said. "Not to worry. They're safely housed in their kennels outdoors at the moment." He made a sort of funny grimace. "No, not to worry. *They* won't be bothering us. . . ."

Basil's keen skills must have picked up on something odd in his tone, for he rounded on the mouse immediately. "What do you mean, sir?"

"I'll tell you in a moment—let's get inside first." Elwood gestured toward a window low to the ground, which stood slightly open—more than enough so for a mouse to enter. "This way, if you please."

Inside, we found ourselves in a lavishly appointed sitting room. Elwood led us across and into the hallway beyond.

"There's a shortcut just through here," he said, gesturing toward another door across the way. "Go on. I'll keep watch."

Keep watch for what? I wondered, thinking once more of the howling hounds outside.

But I squeezed beneath the door and stood— only to find myself facing an absolutely enormous cat with its jaws wide open to reveal gleaming fangs!

3

CATS AND DOGS

"RUN!" I CROAKED OUT, MY LIFE FLASHING BEFORE my eyes as the cat's mouth stretched open even wider. I wasn't sure I could make it back out beneath the door before the slavering creature was upon me, but perhaps at least Basil and Elwood could still escape with their lives. . . .

Behind me, though, Basil merely chuckled as he emerged from beneath the door. "Relax, Dawson," he said. "I don't think you have to worry about this particular feline."

Elwood appeared in time to hear him. He glanced at the cat. "Yes, this is Cecil," he informed me.

"Cecil?" I stared, glassy-eyed with fear, at the cat.

"Cecil, the royal cat." Basil strolled past the creature, which hadn't stirred from its position sprawled on a Persian rug. "It's well known that he has reached a state of détente with the resident mice."

"H-he has?" I realized that the cat had closed its jaws by now. Had he indeed been preparing to eat me—or had it been merely a yawn?

"Basil is correct," Elwood said. "Cecil won't bother chasing us—he's far too lazy."

The cat regarded him with his green eyes held half-open, seeming disinclined to argue with the mouse's assessment. Then he yawned again, rolled over, and stretched. I stared, mesmerized, as he exposed and then retracted the claws on one large, furry paw. Détente or not, I intended to keep my distance from those weapons of death!

"Shall we go?" I said to the others, trying to sound blasé. "I'm sure the duke is waiting."

"This way." Elwood pointed across the room at a mouse-size hole in the wainscoting, informing us that it was the fastest way to the royal mice's quarters. Then he led the way toward it, directly past Cecil.

I followed, still keeping a wary eye on the beast. But Cecil didn't move, aside from a slow twitch of his tail.

Suddenly there was a flurry of barking from just beyond another door in the room, which stood slightly ajar. The door flew open, and a dog rushed in. The creature wasn't much larger than Cecil, with floppy ears and a wiry coat.

I felt slightly relieved, expecting the dog to do what dogs did best—that is, chase cats. Despite Elwood's assurances, I knew I would feel better if Cecil were a bit farther away!

Beside me, I saw Basil stiffen. "Make haste, Dawson," he said, grabbing me by the sleeve. "To the hole—now!"

He nearly yanked me off my feet as he sprinted for the hole. "Wait!" I protested, rather relishing the thought of watching the lazy cat chased from the room.

But I'd long since learned to trust Basil's instincts. And so I allowed him to drag me into the hole in the wainscoting. Elwood was right behind us, in fact giving me a hearty shove as he dove after me into the hole.

"That was close!" he said, his voice shaking slightly.

I frowned, glancing out through the hole—directly into the moist, toothy mouth of the dog! He let out a shrill bark, nearly deafening me.

"Let's get away," Basil told Elwood, raising his voice to be heard above the barks and growls from outside. "Then you can explain."

We hurried along the narrow passage within the walls, around the corner, and out of earshot—at least nearly—of the dog. Then Basil stopped and faced Elwood.

"You said the prince's dogs are outside in the kennels," he said.

Elwood nodded. "I'm sorry. I should have warned you about that one." He shuddered as he glanced back the way we'd just come. "I didn't think we'd encounter him before the duke had a chance to fill you in."

"Why did he ignore the cat to chase us?" I asked, still perplexed by the animal's odd behavior. True, many dogs will pursue mice—but not if there's a cat nearby to be chased instead! I glanced at Basil, realizing something else. "You knew," I told him. "You saw that he was about to come after us. How?"

Basil shrugged one thin shoulder. "Mr. Holmes is very interested in canine behavior and body language—it's come into play in several of his cases," he said, as if that explained anything!

Meanwhile, Elwood was speaking again. "That dog belongs to the Bohemian nobles," he told us. "One of the human princes, a lad named Leo, has a mouse phobia."

I blinked. "He fears mice?" I exclaimed. "How ridiculous! What danger could we pose to a human?"

"I have no idea." Elwood shook his head. "But it's true, I'm afraid. The Bohemian noblemice have explained that they can't let even a whisker show when the humans are around due to Leo's fear and loathing of our kind. He even trained that dog to hunt and kill any mouse he sees!"

I traded a sober look with Basil. We were well accustomed to staying out of sight of humans, of course—all mice were. Many of them could be a bit funny about sharing their food, water, and homes with us. But it was an uncomfortable feeling to think of a human hating mousekind so much that he would train a dog to kill us!

"That's what I was referring to earlier," Elwood went on. "The prince has kenneled his own dogs outside, since they're so much larger than the visiting canine, and Prince Leo takes his pet with him everywhere."

"How terrible to have to live with a creature like that," I mused, thinking of the Bohemian noblemice. "The local royals are lucky indeed that Cecil poses no threat to them."

Elwood smiled slightly. "Indeed. Now, come— let's meet the duke and his family, and they can fill you in on the rest."

A ROYAL
PROBLEM

THE DUKE WAS A TALL, STOUT MOUSE WITH GRAY whiskers, and the duchess, a lovely older lady with perfect manners. They stood at the front of a delegation of nearly twenty mice that emerged to meet us in a roomy, comfortably appointed space in the wall behind the humans' drawing room. Most were members of the duke's family and associated servants, while a few oddly dressed mice were introduced as the Bohemian visitors.

"Thank you for coming," the duke told Basil somberly once all introductions had been made. "If you are ready to hear of the terrible dilemma that has brought you here, I am ready to share it."

"You are most welcome, Your Grace." Basil's sharp gaze scanned the group of mice gathered behind the duke and duchess. "But I suspect I might already have guessed what is wrong."

"Oh?" The duke raised his brow in the direction of Elwood.

"No, Your Grace." Basil held up a paw. "Elwood was the soul of discretion. He hasn't told me a thing. However, my powers of observation are telling me that you have introduced me to adult mice of all ages, along with several younger children." He patted the head of a wide-eyed little girl from the Bohemian delegation, then glanced at an even younger pup playing with the tassels of the rug. "However, I see no teenage mice at all—though I am aware that your son, daughter, and niece are all within this age range."

The duke looked surprised. "I see that your reputation is well-founded, sir. Yes, you have struck upon the issue at paw."

The duchess nodded, wringing a silk handkerchief between her paws. "Our guests brought along four teenagers of their own," she began. "All seven youngsters struck up an immediate friendship."

"That is correct," the duke said with a nod. "But like all youngsters of their age, they concocted some rather, er, unusual forms of fun."

The Mouse King of Bohemia stepped forward. "Yes, I am afraid my eldest son, Marek, struck upon the idea," he said in exotically accented but otherwise perfect English. "The youngsters have been setting dares for one another."

"Often involving Pes," his wife, the queen, added with a shudder.

"Pes?" I said.

"I expect that is the name of the dog we just

encountered," Basil told me, stroking his chin thoughtfully.

"Why, yes!" Elwood spoke up, surprised. "I didn't think I'd told you the beast's name."

Basil smiled. "You didn't. But I find it helpful to know a smattering of other languages. And 'Pes' is the Bohemian word for 'dog,' is it not, Your Majesty?" he said, addressing the last bit to the king.

"Yes," the king said, seeming impressed—as was I, for Basil's breadth of knowledge often surprised even his best friend!

The duchess was still twisting her kerchief anxiously. "We do not know what the latest dare might have been," she told Basil and me. "But the teens have disappeared without a trace, and I fear something has gone terribly awry. . . ." She allowed her voice to trail off, though tears glistened in her dark eyes.

"Please, madam, try not to fret." Basil bowed to her, then scanned the entire group. "May I have leave to question everyone here?"

"Of course," the duke said at once, and the king nodded his assent.

"What can I do to help, Basil?" I asked.

He regarded me briefly. "Nothing for the moment, Dawson," he said. "If you can, try to reassure the ladies that now that I'm on the case, the fate of their offspring shall soon be known, for better or for worse."

I wasn't sure I wished to share that last bit with the ladies. But I did my best to obey the first portion of Basil's command. I spent the next half hour or more chatting with the duchess, the queen, and several other ladies while Basil circled the room, talking to each mouse in turn. I couldn't hear much of his questioning, though I heard enough to understand that he was inquiring what they knew of the dares completed thus far, along with the mysterious final one that seemingly had led to the disappearance.

Finally, Basil asked for attention. "I have some good news for you," he told the assembled anxious mice. "The teen noblemice may indeed be missing, and I have no idea as of yet where they may be."

"That's good news?" the duchess asked in surprise.

Basil smiled. "Indeed it is," he said. "For wherever your children may be, I can assure you that they're *not* in the belly of the beast."

THE SEARCH
BEGINS

THERE WAS A CLAMOR OF VOICES AS THE ROYALS asked questions and exclaimed over what Basil had just said. Finally the duke raised a paw for silence.

"Please, sir," he said, addressing Basil with an air of slight skepticism. "How can you assure us of any such thing?"

The king nodded. "With all due respect, we know this creature Pes much better than we might wish." He glanced at the other Bohemians. "The dog is a terror, with no compunction about pursuing any mouse he can find."

"He nearly bit my tail off just weeks ago!" exclaimed another Bohemian royal, a cousin of the queen's who had been introduced as Ladislav.

Basil waited patiently, paws tucked behind his back, for the clamor to subside again. "If you will allow me, I shall tell you how I can assure you of exactly that," he said. "You see, Dawson and I received a rather close-up look at Pes on our way here."

Elwood grimaced. "My apologies again, dear sirs."

"No need for that." Basil held up a paw in protest. "For as luck would have it, that close encounter provided me with a good look at our prime suspect. And I saw no signs of blood, fur, or other evidence around his mouth and teeth."

"Oh my!" the King of Bohemia exclaimed, fanning himself with his paw.

Basil ignored the reaction. "The dog also acted rather frustrated, telling me that he hasn't had a successful hunt in a long time."

"However do you know so much about dog behavior, sir?" the duchess asked.

Basil glanced at me and winked. "It's all thanks to my mentor—Mr. Sherlock Holmes," he said. "But never mind that. Many of you mentioned that

you searched the castle for the youngsters before summoning me, yes?"

"That is right," Ladislav said, while others nodded. "We searched everywhere with no luck at all."

Basil nodded. "That clinches it. While a murderous cat might carry away its prize, dogs are generally rather messy hunters. If Pes had caught your children, there would be evidence at the scene of the crime."

"And we would have spotted that terrible evidence during our search," Ladislav said, nodding as well. "I see! Very logical. But, then, what has happened to them?"

"Could it be . . . ?" I hesitated, not wanting to put my chilling thought into words. "Er, could Cecil be our culprit?"

The duke chuckled. "No need to worry about that, sir," he told me. "Cecil is far too lazy to chase even one fat old mouse, let alone seven fit youngsters!"

Several of the other royals chuckled and agreed, leaving me certain that my theory was well worth discarding.

Basil's pronouncement had quieted some of the adults' fears. But they remained concerned. Where could the teens be, and why hadn't they yet returned from their latest adventure?

"That's what I aim to find out," Basil told them. "I shall analyze the information at paw and work backward toward a solution."

"Work backward?" the Queen of Bohemia echoed. "What do you mean?"

"I'll need someone to take me to the last place the teens were seen," Basil replied.

Ladislav raised a paw at once. "I can take them," he said.

A cheerful British earl named George volunteered to come as well. "After all, you'll need a local to help you get around this big old house," he said.

"I'll come as well, if that's all right?" Elwood spoke up, glancing at the duke, who nodded. "Let's depart at once!"

"Be careful, all of you," the duke said.

"And let us know what you find," the duchess added. "I'm dreadfully worried about the youngsters—perhaps the boys might forget the time in their mischief, but my dear daughter, Clara, would never stay away so long without reason."

I joined the group as well, of course. The five of us took our leave, heading out of the room into the dark space between the walls. We scurried up pipes and through holes, making our way across the great house. Finally George held up a paw.

"This is the place," he whispered. "Isn't that right, Ladislav?"

The Bohemian royal nodded. "I last saw my cousin Marek in there. He was joining the other teens for another prank, though he would not tell me what was planned."

Basil peered out through a mouse-size hole in the wall. "Interesting," he murmured.

"What is it, Basil?" I looked out as well—and my eyes widened with alarm. The room before us appeared to be some kind of human dining area, with a long table at the center and several chairs and sofas scattered about.

Lounging upon one of the sofas was a young human boy—and the beast Pes sat at his feet! The dog was gnawing on a scrap of blue-dyed fur stuffed with straw, which I took to be some sort of chew toy.

The others looked out and saw the pair too. "That's Prince Leo," Ladislav told us. "And, of course, you are already acquainted with Pes. . . ."

I grimaced. "What are they doing?"

"Use your powers of observation, dear Dawson," Basil said. "There is a tray of sugary pastries—nearly empty. I deduce that the tray has been there since breakfast, and that Prince Leo has returned to have one more before it is taken away by the servants."

I saw that he was right. Leo was munching on a pastry matching the few left on the tray. I'm not ashamed to admit that the sight made my mouth

water a little—after all, Elwood's sudden arrival had interrupted our breakfast!

"Don't get too close to the hole," George warned. "Otherwise that blasted dog might—"

The rest of his words were lost in a flurry of loud barking, for Pes suddenly leaped to his feet and raced toward us. Even though I knew a sturdy wall stood between us and the beast, it took all my courage not to turn tail and run.

Pes skidded to a stop in front of the hole, sniffing away with his huge, moist nose. Then he barked again.

"Come." Elwood sounded anxious. "We should

be away before the human boy comes to investigate."

"Oh dear." I glanced at my friend. "This case might be trickier than expected with that creature hanging around, eh, Basil?"

A slight smile played at the corners of his muzzle. "Perhaps, Dawson," he replied. "But it's off to a fine start regardless of the dog's presence. I've just spotted a clue!"

A CLUE!

"A CLUE?" ELWOOD EXCLAIMED. "WHAT IS IT, SIR?"

Basil pointed to the floor at our feet. "There," he said. "Paw prints!"

I leaned closer, squinting in the dim light within the walls. The others did the same.

"By Jove, you're right!" George exclaimed.

Now I saw the prints too. They were white, clearly left by paws that had trodden in the sugar on that pastry tray!

"Observe the size." Basil stepped closer, measuring the prints against his own foot. "Smaller than an adult mouse—which means they were likely left by our missing teens."

Ladislav shot him an admiring look. "Well deduced, sir," he said. "Let's follow them and see where they lead!"

"Exactly my thinking, my dear sir." Basil led the way along the trail of paw prints.

I hurried after him. "I expect that dog scared off the teens while they were helping themselves to the pastries," I guessed. "That means they might be just ahead of us!"

"I'm afraid it's more likely these prints were made some time ago, Dawson," Basil said. "The pastries smelled rather stale, which means they've

36

been there for some time—perhaps since the earliest breakfast service this morning."

"Oh." My heart sank as I realized we might not be as close as I'd hoped to finding the teens.

The trail of sugary paw prints led us down several narrow corridors within the walls, then finally to another hidey-hole in the wainscoting. This one opened into a very large room filled with bustling human servants.

"That's the ballroom," Elwood informed us.

George nodded. "The humans are hosting a grand royal ball tomorrow evening, with their Bohemian visitors as the guests of honor."

I peeked out again. A human maid hurried past with a broom, soon followed by a servant carrying several stacked chairs.

Basil was surveying the room. "I say," he exclaimed, his gaze settling on a large item near the center of the room. "That's a fine-looking photographic camera the humans have set up! Quite modern!"

"Yes, the Prince of Wales is very proud of it," Elwood said. "He's been capturing images of the visitors since their arrival last week. I believe he plans to develop and present the photographs to them at the ball as a memento of the visit."

I stared at the camera with great curiosity. It consisted of a large wooden cabinet with a door set into it. Atop that was the camera machine itself, a mystifying contraption I could make neither head nor tail of. The whole thing was as tall as a man and nearly as wide.

"Yes, very nice," Basil murmured, sounding impressed. "A gelatin dry plate machine, if I'm not mistaken—very advanced indeed."

"It sounds as if you have an interest in photography, Basil," George commented.

Basil shrugged and turned away. "I have an interest in many things, sir," he replied. "But never mind—we must continue the search."

"How?" Elwood peered out at the ballroom. "The humans are already hard at work sweeping the floor. The trail of paw prints ends here!"

THE END OF
THE TRAIL?

NOW WHAT? WITH NO TRAIL OF PAW PRINTS TO follow and no other clue within sight, I was at a loss. Fortunately, however, Basil rarely finds himself in such a state. He was staring across the ballroom with keenly narrowed eyes.

"Observe—Cecil has just entered," he commented.

Elwood barely spared the cat a glance. "Don't worry. He won't trouble us—or the teens, even if he happens to stumble across them."

George chuckled. "Indeed."

But Basil was still watching the royal feline. "All evidence points to the truth of your assertion that Cecil has no interest in chasing mice," he said. "However, he is still a cat—with a cat's instincts. And from the moment he entered the room, he has been staring at the camera!"

I saw that he was right. Cecil had seated himself in a sunny spot on the floor. The servants were forced to dodge around him as they hurried about their work. But the cat paid no attention to any of the humans. His green eyes were trained on the large box camera at the center of the room.

"That is strange," I commented. "Why is he staring so?"

Basil smiled. "Because that is where the young noblemice are hiding," he exclaimed. "I'd wager my last crumb of cheese on it!"

Ladislav looked surprised. "Do you really think so? Why would they hide in such a place?"

"We shall ask them exactly that question after we rescue them," Basil replied.

"Rescue them—but how?" Elwood said.

I saw his concern. As previously mentioned, the camera stood in the center of the room, with no other furniture, rug, or other possible hiding place anywhere nearby. With at least a dozen humans rushing around preparing for the ball, how would we ever reach the teens?

George looked dejected. "I suppose the teens will have to continue hiding until nightfall," he said. "Surely the humans will depart then, and the youngsters can make their way home."

"No need to wait." Basil had a certain look in his eye that I recognized at once. He was concocting a plan!

"What are you thinking, Basil?" I asked.

He didn't answer for a moment. I caught Elwood and George trading a confused look. Ladislav was still watching Cecil, who continued to stare at the camera.

Finally Basil smiled. "I've got it," he announced. He spun and pointed to Elwood. "You—you've already proven yourself fast and brave. . . ."

A DARING PLAN

I COULDN'T HELP FEELING WORRIED AS WE PUT Basil's plan into action. Elwood had been eager to volunteer for a key part once he'd heard what the great detective had in mind. But would it work? Was it too dangerous? I dared not try to imagine all the possible ways it could go wrong.

"Do you see him yet?" George whispered, peering out into the ballroom.

"He'll probably come in through that door." Basil pointed across the cavernous room. "It's standing open, see?"

I did, and I was about to say so when a small

blue blur entered the room—followed by a wildly barking Pes!

"Here he comes!" Ladislav cried.

I held my breath, watching the blue dog toy. To the humans it probably looked as if Pes had batted the thing into the room and was now chasing after it. But we mice knew the truth—Elwood had yanked the straw out of the chew toy and then pulled the blue fabric over himself as a disguise. It was his scurrying feet propelling the toy into and around the ballroom!

Shouts erupted from humans all around the room as Elwood dashed beneath a maid's cleaning cart. The pursuing Pes crashed into it, nearly tipping it over. Then he pranced around, barking madly and trying to dive under the cart, though he was far too big to fit.

"No! Naughty dog!" one of the servants scolded. "Grab him, someone!"

"Careful," a maid called out. "Prince Leo adores that little monster. Don't hurt him or there will be trouble."

Several servants descended on Pes, who ignored them as he continued to bark and try to reach Elwood. The rest of the humans paused in their work to watch.

"They're properly distracted now," Basil hissed. "Let's go!"

The four of us dashed out of our hidey-hole. My legs felt weak with terror as I realized the mouse-hunting dog was only a few yards away. Luckily, however, his attention remained fully on the cleaning cart.

We made it to the box camera without being noticed. There was a small hole in the bottom, more than large enough for a mouse to squeeze through. Seconds later we were inside the cabinet.

But we found it rather crowded, for huddled within were seven teenage mice!

"Cousin Ladislav!" a young teen girl cried, flinging herself at the mouse in question. "Did you come to rescue us?"

"That is right, Silvie," Ladislav replied. "Thanks to the great detective Basil of Baker Street, who solved the mystery of where to find you!"

A handsome older teen bowed to Basil. "Many thanks, sir," he said. "I am Marek, prince of Bohemia."

There were two more Bohemian royals as well, a younger lad named Radim and an older girl, Marek's sister, known as Pavla. The British youngsters included Clara, the daughter of the duke and duchess, her brother, Hugo, and their cousin, Florrie.

I glanced around the cabinet. A few crumbs of that sugary pastry littered the pile of glass photographic plates upon which the young mice had been sitting.

"I see that you haven't been hungry, at least," I said with a smile, my own stomach rumbling slightly at the memory of my interrupted breakfast.

"No, but we've been dreadfully frightened!" Florrie exclaimed. "And besides that . . ." She hesitated, glancing at the other teens.

"What is it, Florrie?" George asked. "What's wrong? You're safe now."

"Perhaps not," Marek said grimly. "You see, something terrible has happened!"

A CURIOUS
CONFESSION

"EXPLAIN," BASIL DEMANDED. THEN HE PEERED OUT
into the ballroom. "No—wait. You can explain
once we're safely back in the walls. Come with
me—quickly!"

He leaped out of the camera cabinet. I followed,
along with the others. A maid was just passing,
dressed in a voluminous floor-length black skirt.
Basil dashed beneath the skirt, and we followed,
scurrying along while carefully keeping clear of
the woman's clunky black shoes as she crossed
the room. In that way, we stayed hidden from the
humans, who had by now removed both Pes and
Cecil from the room. Once we came close enough

to the hidey-hole, we dashed out from under the skirt and were safe again. By the time we arrived, Elwood was already waiting for us, breathless and with his furry blue disguise abandoned outside.

"Good work, sir," Basil told him. Then he turned to the teenagers once more. "Explain," he repeated. "What terrible thing has happened, other than worrying your families half to death?"

"We're sorry about that." Clara's face looked drawn and anxious. "We didn't mean to make them worry."

Marek nodded. "It's just that we took our last dare a step too far," he added.

"Yes." Clara glared at him. "It was his idea."

Marek shrugged. "I admit it. I overheard a human saying that the royal family—ours, that is"—here he glanced at the other Bohemians—"would be sitting for a photographic portrait in the breakfast room first thing this morning."

"So he dared us to pop up behind them as the photograph was taken," his sister, Pavla, went on. "That way we would appear in the photograph—with the humans none the wiser!"

I couldn't help smiling. It was a clever plan indeed! "And then what happened?" I asked, kicking at a bit of sugar still lingering on the floor nearby. "Did you pull it off?"

"Of course." Young Hugo puffed out his chest with pride. "We hid until just the right moment, then posed behind the humans' shoulders. None of them noticed a thing—not even the photographer!"

Marek grinned for a second. Then his shoulders slumped. "But then we heard that this photo would be presented at the ball tomorrow night," he said. "That's when we realized our terrible mistake."

I blinked, not sure what he meant. But Basil was nodding.

"I see," he said. "When that photograph is unveiled, someone is sure to spot the mice in the background."

"Yes," Clara said worriedly. "And given Prince Leo's hatred of mice . . ."

"The humans are likely to stop at nothing to drive all mice out of Marlborough House," her cousin Florrie finished for her.

"To say nothing of how we will ever get home," Marek added. "Leo's father insisted he keep Pes caged for most of the journey here. But if he thinks there could be mice about . . ."

"He's likely to give the beast free rein of the carriages and ship, just in case," Pavla finished grimly.

"Oh dear," I said, finally seeing the problem.

All the teens looked worried. But Prince Marek forced a smile. "Worst of all," he said, "they're likely to lock up their stores of my favorite delicious Abertam cheese!"

"Abertam, eh?" I licked my chops, hungrier than ever at the mention of cheese. "I don't think I've tried that one."

"It's a Bohemian specialty," Basil told me absently. "But never mind that, Dawson. We have more important things than cheese to occupy our minds at the moment."

That was easy for him to say! I was about to mention as much when his next words drove all other thoughts from my mind:

"We must get our paws on that photographic plate!" he cried.

10

SEARCH AND DESTROY MISSION

"WE THOUGHT ABOUT THAT," MAREK TOLD BASIL glumly. "That's why we ended up hiding in the camera. We hoped to find the plate there and destroy or smudge it somehow."

Clara nodded. "But the camera cabinet contains only unexposed plates," she said. "The others must already have been taken to the darkroom."

"Oh dear," I said. "It could already be too late!"

Basil shook his head firmly. "Nonsense, Dawson," he said. "If that photograph had already been developed, the search for the mice would be on by now."

"That's true," young Silvie agreed. "The humans

wouldn't be shooing Pes away as a nuisance—they would be encouraging him!"

"Correct," Basil said with an approving nod for the youngster. "That means we still have time."

I realized he was right. The ball wasn't until the following evening— more than twenty-four hours hence. We did have time, at least a little. . . .

"All we have to do is find that plate," Basil declared, pacing back and forth in the limited space between the walls. "Then we can spirit it off if possible, or at least break the glass so it's ruined." He stopped and spun to face Clara. "Now, where is the humans' darkroom?"

Clara and Hugo traded a look. "It's at the opposite end of the house from where we stand now," Hugo said.

Princess Clara sighed. "If only we hadn't agreed to that stupid prank!"

"You might as well come out and say it—you blame me!" Marek snapped, glaring at her.

She returned his hostile expression. "You're right. I do blame you," she retorted. "I knew you were a show-off!"

"That's enough," Basil said, silencing them.

"We'll need our wits about us if we're to fix this. There's no time to waste in sniping at each other."

"Sorry," Marek mumbled, while Clara just shrugged and turned away, frowning.

"We'd better set off at once for the darkroom," Elwood suggested. "It's this way. . . ."

As we followed him through the walls, I leaned closer to Basil. "Marek and Clara don't seem to get along too well," I murmured. "I hope their obvious distaste for each other doesn't cause an international incident to add to our problems!"

As promised, the journey across the massive house was a long one. We crept through walls, across vacant rooms, and up and down pipes and molding.

The trip seemed to take longer than it might have otherwise, since the teens kept moaning and worrying aloud over what they'd done. Marek and Clara, in particular, found every opportunity to blame each other for what had happened and otherwise show their disdain for the other.

But I did my best to ignore all that and focus on the case at hand, just as I imagined Basil—or Mr. Holmes himself—might advise. I suspected we would need all our strength, mental and physical alike, once we reached the darkroom.

After nearly an hour's travel, George paused and peered out through a hidey-hole. "Here," he said. "We can take a shortcut through the prince's study."

"Are you certain?" Elwood sounded worried. "At this time of the evening he's usually in there."

Young Hugo shrugged. "He's not there now," he said, peering out to make sure of it. "Besides, his dogs are banished to the kennels while the visitors are here, remember? It's safe enough."

Elwood nodded, and the rest of us took him at his word—especially once he mentioned that the shortcut would subtract at least fifteen minutes' scurrying off our journey.

George led the way out of the wainscoting into the large but cozy study, which was filled with comfortable leather furniture, dark paneling, worn but luxurious rugs, and wooden cabinets full of trophies, glassware, and other items.

We were about halfway across the room when the door opened—and Pes raced in, barking like mad as he careened toward us!

11

A TERRIFYING ATTACK

WE WERE ONLY A YARD FROM THE NEAREST WALL, with an inviting hidey-hole visible. "Run!" George cried, flinging himself in that direction.

Most of the group followed, including myself. But I paused and glanced back, realizing that Basil wasn't beside me.

Indeed, he had stopped to look back as well, and I soon saw why—Clara stood frozen with terror, staring wide-eyed and pale as Pes lunged toward her!

"Clara!" Basil shouted, diving toward her.

Swallowing my terror, I followed, grabbing one of her arms as Basil took the other. In that

way, we lifted her bodily between us, tossing her into a sturdy wooden cabinet through a missing pane in its glass doors and then following her ourselves. A second later came the thump and rattle of Pes flinging himself against the cabinet, though his barking was somewhat muffled by the glass and wood.

I collapsed onto the cool glass cabinet floor,

shaking with fear at our near miss. "I—I'm sorry!" Clara cried. "I don't know what happened. I just couldn't move. . . ."

"It's all right, miss," Basil told her. "The mind can play funny tricks upon one at moments of great stress. It's quite natural."

"Do you think the others got away?" she exclaimed. "What if that terrible dog caught them?"

She went quite pale and shaky, presumably concerned about the well-being of her brother and cousin. But Basil quickly reassured her.

"The others most certainly escaped—you can count on it," he said with great conviction. "Otherwise that beast wouldn't be trying to get at us."

"Oh! That's true." Looking much relieved, Clara sat down and leaned against a bottle to catch her breath. Meanwhile, I looked around. We appeared to be in some sort of large cabinet containing fancy glass bottles filled with liquids of various hues, along with vessels of different shapes from which to drink them.

Outside, two humans had hurried into the room as well, perhaps drawn by the dog's frenzied barking.

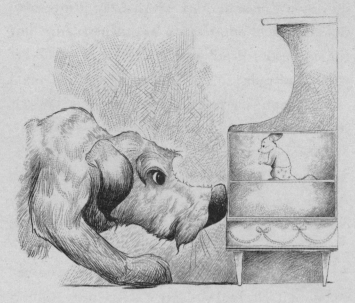

"Pes, no!" the smaller of the two—Prince Leo, as I could see when I pressed my face to the frosted glass—shouted, pulling the dog away from the cabinet. He added a few more words in what I could only assume was his native tongue.

"I say, what a racket," commented the larger human. My eyes widened as I realized who it was— the Prince of Wales himself, Edward, second-eldest child of Queen Victoria and the master of this house!

I didn't hear the rest of what the prince said. But a moment later he and Leo departed, pulling the study door firmly shut behind them—with Pes still on our side!

"Oh dear," Clara said, peering out at the dog. He was prowling around the cabinet, sniffing for a way in. "They've locked that creature in here with us!"

"Yes. Leaving no obvious path of escape until they return for him." Basil seemed disgruntled— an unusual state for him. "As I've mentioned, Mr. Holmes often uses canine behavior to aid him in his cases, but this particular beast seems to exist only to hinder mine!"

Clara nodded. "It's hard to imagine, isn't it?" she said softly.

Basil didn't seem to hear her, having drifted into deep thought. But I smiled at the girl kindly. "What's that, miss?"

She shrugged. "It's hard to imagine life in a place with such a dog around all the time," she said. "Especially after growing up here, with lazy Cecil."

Basil suddenly snapped back to attention. "Now that we've a moment to catch our breath," he said, "why don't you tell me about that photograph. Every detail—leave nothing out."

I was surprised by his questioning. "What difference do such details make, Basil?" I asked. "All we need to do is find and then break the blasted plate, after all."

Basil shrugged. "No knowledge is wasted, Dawson." He nodded at Clara. "Please—tell me everything."

She did so, running out of descriptive words after about fifteen minutes. For another three quarters of an hour or more, we sat in near silence.

Well, Clara and I sat. Basil paced incessantly, dodging between decanter and glass, then past several cloudy bottles before making the turn at the end and stalking past us, over and over.

By the time a full hour had passed, my stomach was grumbling loudly enough for Clara to hear. She offered me a shy smile—and then a scrap of cheese pulled from her pocket.

"Here," she said. "Take this. It sounds as if you haven't eaten in a while."

"Are you sure?" I said, my stomach growling anew at the delectable scent of it. "There's no

telling how long we'll be in here. You might want
to keep it for yourself."

"It's all right. I'm not hungry." She held out the
cheese. "Please, take it."

I needed no third invitation, gobbling the cheese
greedily. "Mmm," I said. "Delicious! But what is it?
I've never tasted a cheese quite like it before."

Basil stalked past again just in time to hear me.
"It's a ripe Abertam, of course," he said. "That's
the Bohemian cheese young Prince Marek mentioned as a particular favorite of his. The scent is
quite distinctive." He paused in his pacing, staring
at Clara. "Did the prince give it to you?"

"No!" she blurted out quickly, blushing. "Er . . .

I mean, of course not. Why would you assume such a thing? It was, um, his sister, Pavla."

Basil stared at her, then nodded. "I see," he said, and then resumed his pacing.

I licked the last crumb of cheese off my paw, then settled myself to wait. For how long? I could only guess. . . .

THE LONG WAIT

AN UNKNOWN PERIOD OF TIME LATER, I AWOKE with a start when Basil shook me by the shoulder.

"Wake up, Dawson," he said. "Someone has just entered."

I sat up, yawning and trying to catch my bearings. Nearby, Clara looked sleepy too, though Basil was wide-awake and peering out through the broken pane in the cabinet door.

I joined him there. "It's Leo!" I whispered.

Sure enough, the human lad had just entered the study. "Pes!" he called, adding a whistle and a few words in his own language.

The dog pricked an ear toward the boy but

stayed where he was, on alert in front of the cabinet where we hid. Leo frowned, looking annoyed.

"Get over here," he said. "You are already in trouble for disrupting the cleaning of the ballroom earlier. Now you wish to make trouble in the prince's study as well?" He stepped forward. "Hmm . . . unless perhaps you've found a—a mouse?" His voice trembled slightly on the last word.

"Quick—hide!" Basil hissed, giving me a sudden shove.

The three of us scurried to the back of the cabinet, huddling behind an especially large decanter of dark, sour-smelling liquid.

A second later the cabinet door swung open. Leo peered in, looking nervous. Pes pranced around just behind him, clearly hoping for a chance to leap inside.

"Stay back," the human child warned the dog. "We cannot have you breaking the prince's things. I shall check for—for mice."

With a gulp, he reached forward, tipping up a glass to look inside. He then moved several of the bottles. Would he find us? And if so, would we be able to escape before his killer dog set upon us?

"If he lifts this bottle, run that way," I whispered to Clara, pointing. "Basil and I will distract him while you break for the wall."

"No!" she cried softly. "I can't leave you here to—"

"Hush!" Basil said. "The boy is afraid—he won't dare reach this far in."

As it happened, he was right. After peeking into a few more glasses and behind another bottle or two, Leo gave up and swung the door shut.

"I don't see anything," he told his dog. "So let's go."

But Pes dodged him when he tried to grab his collar. The prince made one more attempt, then let out an exasperated sigh.

"Stay here if you choose, then!" he exclaimed, stomping toward the door.

"Oh no!" I said as I realized we were once again trapped in the room with Pes. "Now what?"

Basil shrugged. "Now we wait."

And so we did. We waited as the shadows in the room grew long and the sky darkened outside. I hoped that Pes might become bored and curl up to sleep, giving us a chance to escape. But he remained on alert, circling the cabinet nonstop.

Eventually I felt my eyes grow heavy. Clara was already sound asleep, curled up inside a short, heavy glass. I found a comfortable spot of my own and was soon snoring away.

When I next opened my eyes, bright daylight was pouring in through the windows. For a moment I thought Basil must have woken me again, for he was standing nearby.

But then I heard the rumbling voice of the Prince of Wales outside and realized it must have been his entrance that had pulled me out of my slumber. "What are you still doing in here, you rascal?" the prince was exclaiming, sounding half-amused and half-annoyed. "Look at the mess you've made! Out with you now!"

"Quick!" Basil said to me and Clara, the latter of whom had apparently awakened before I did. "This is our chance."

As soon as the prince turned to toss the little dog out of his study, we leaped out through the broken pane and sprinted for the wainscoting. Seconds later we were safely back within the walls.

"Hurry!" Basil said, not giving us a chance to

celebrate. "We have to get back to the others and find out if any progress has been made on my plan."

Luckily, Clara knew the way home. But our luck ended there, for when we reached the rest of the royal clans, they had some bad news for us.

"We continued on to the darkroom without you," George told Basil. "But when we got there, we found no way in."

I blinked in surprise, wondering if he was joking. "But we're mice," I said with a half laugh. "We can get in anywhere!"

Elwood shook his head grimly. "Not that darkroom," he told me. "Those royal photographs are so important to the prince that the photographer is taking no chances of having them ruined by a stray bit of light. He's blocked every last nook and cranny so that not even a cockroach could squeeze in!"

13

THE DARKROOM

I GLANCED AT BASIL IN ALARM. BUT HE SEEMED unsurprised by the bad news. "I expected that this might happen," he said calmly. "But no human room is completely mouseproof. We'll have to search harder for a way in, that's all."

He enlisted the older teens—Marek, Clara, Pavla, and Hugo—to help, along with Elwood and George. "Be careful," the duke said as we set off. "The humans are frantically preparing for tonight's ball—they won't be watching where they step."

"And they'll have little patience for mice, should they spot you," his wife added. "They won't want anything to spoil the big night."

70

I nodded, realizing that the ball was only hours away by now. We would have to work fast—if it wasn't already too late!

"What if the photographer is already developing the plates?" I asked Basil as we hurried along.

Marek heard me. "He isn't," he said. "At least not as of an hour ago. I think the humans want to take another photograph or two first."

"Good," Basil said. "But there's no time to waste. Let's move faster!"

We obeyed, speeding through the house as quickly as possible—though we did bypass the shortcut through the prince's study this time!

Finally we reached the darkroom. As the others had warned, it seemed airtight. "Now what?" George wondered helplessly.

Basil glanced at the teens. "You're young, sharp-eyed, and resourceful," he said. "Find me a way in."

I had my doubts about this plan, which seemed like no plan at all. But the teens set off eagerly, and within moments there was a shout.

"I found it!" Hugo cried, hanging from the molding halfway up a corner of the wall. "Look—a pipe leading right into the darkroom!"

"Good work, lad," Basil said. "It looks like a ventilation pipe of some sort."

I climbed up to examine it. "It's barely big enough for a mouse to squeeze through," I pointed out. "We'll never be able to bring out that photographic plate this way."

Basil shrugged. "Then we'll have to break it instead. I'll need . . . hmm, perhaps three of you to come with me to help push it off the table."

"I'll go!" Elwood volunteered at once.

"Me too," Clara said.

Marek shook his head. "You're not strong enough," he told her. "Stay here—I'll go instead."

Clara frowned. "Who says I'm not strong enough?"

"I do," Basil interrupted. "I'm sorry, miss, but you're the smallest of all of us. Marek shall accompany me, along with Elwood and Dawson."

Clara looked ready to argue, but Basil didn't wait around to hear it. The four of us were soon crawling through the tight pipe into the darkroom, leaving George, Hugo, Pavla, and Clara behind to keep watch.

The place was well named. Even though mice

can see better in the dark than humans, I was hard-pressed to see much at all at first. But my eyes adjusted quickly, and I could make out the dimensions of a small, narrow room. There was a high counter along one wall with a chair before it. Upon the countertop were several bins and dishes, though I didn't focus on those, having eyes only for a stack of glass plates on the floor near the door.

Elwood saw them too. "Oh no!" he exclaimed. "The plates are on the floor!"

"Now what can we do?" I said, for our plan had relied upon gravity to help us break the plate by pushing it from a high place onto the hard floor.

"Maybe we should call the others in," Marek suggested. "With all of us helping, we might be able to carry it up to the countertop. . . ."

Just then the door opened, allowing in a dazzling shaft of light from the hallway outside. Half-blinded by the sudden brightness, we scurried to hide behind a box.

The photographer entered, switched on a dim gas light, and closed the door behind him. Then he reached for the top plate on the stack and lifted it up, away, out of our sight on the counter above.

"He must be starting the development process," Elwood hissed. "We're out of time!"

Marek peered at the stack of plates. "At least he didn't begin with the photograph we're in," he whispered. "It's fourth in the stack, I think."

"What should we do now, Basil?" I whispered fearfully, hoping the photographer didn't shift his position and spot us.

Basil looked thoughtful in the dim, flickering light. "Go outside, Dawson. Take the others with you. I've just concocted a plan B."

"Really?" My heart leaped with hope. "What is it?"

"There's no time to explain." Basil glanced around at the three of us. "And hold on—actually, I'll need one mouse to stay and assist me."

I expected him to choose me, but instead he pointed at the young Bohemian prince. "Marek, you stay," he ordered. "Dawson and Elwood, go on— and tell the others we'll join you in a few minutes."

I did as he said, feeling perplexed and slightly insulted—but hopeful that, once again, the great Basil of Baker Street would somehow find a way to triumph in the face of a seemingly hopeless challenge. . . .

14

THE ROYAL BALL

A COUPLE OF HOURS LATER, I STILL WASN'T SURE whether or not Basil had pulled it off. He and Marek had emerged from the pipe after about twenty minutes, looking confident but refusing to tell the rest of us a thing.

"Don't worry, Dawson," Basil had told me. "You'll find out what we did soon enough—and we'll all find out whether it worked."

That didn't ease my mind much. But I had little choice but to wait and wonder.

Soon it was time for the human ball to begin. We mice hid in the ballroom wall and watched as the humans swept in, dressed in their fancy clothes and laughing and talking more loudly than usual. Cecil was there too—someone had even knotted a jaunty bow tie around his furry neck, which he scratched at occasionally but seemed otherwise too lazy to worry about.

The band struck up a lively tune, and the humans began to dance. Then Pes raced in, barking loudly, as usual. Cecil stiffened, then escaped the dog by jumping atop one of the small tables set around the edges of the room.

"Dash it all," the duke exclaimed. "There goes any hope of sneaking out and helping ourselves to the refreshments."

I nodded, disappointed, since I'd barely recovered from my long bout of hunger after my interrupted breakfast. But the royal mice had brought along plenty of refreshments of their own, and soon we were all enjoying tasty cheese and other delicacies.

Outside, the human royals began raising their glasses to toast the visit. We did the same.

"We'll miss having you around," the duke told the Bohemian mouse king fondly. "I hope you'll come back to visit soon."

"I hope so too." The king nibbled a bit of cracker. "I wonder if the humans feel the same."

The duke peered out through the hidey-hole. "They appear fond enough of one another, despite the presence of that infernal canine."

I had to agree. I expected the prince and his family would indeed miss their charming, worldly visitors—just as the British mice of the house would miss their Bohemian counterparts.

Well, most of them would, anyway . . . At that moment I caught a glimpse of Clara and Marek. They were a little way down the narrow corridor, staring at each other with a tense look about them.

But I had little time to wonder what they were arguing about this time, for the duke let out a cry. "They're about to reveal the photos!"

I clustered at the hidey-hole with the others, holding my breath. The Prince of Wales had just stepped to the center of the room. He stood smiling, facing the visiting Bohemian monarch.

"Your attention, please," the prince called out. "I have something special to present to our esteemed guests—a memento suited to the honor of their visit."

He gestured to someone off to the side, and the photographer stepped forward holding a stack of framed photographs.

The humans *ooh*ed and *aah*ed as he held them up one by one, with the prince offering jocular comments on each captured moment. Finally he reached the family photo—the one we'd spent so much time and effort trying to prevent from being developed. What had Basil done?

When the photographer held up that photo, a gasp went up from the humans—and from us mice as well. For there, smudging half the photo, was a paw print!

"I'm sorry, sire," the photographer said. "That paw mark was on the plate. There was nothing I

could do to salvage the rest of the photo."

"Ah," the duke said, turning to smile at Basil. "He couldn't salvage the rest—namely, the part featuring our mischievous offspring!"

Basil winked, leaving little doubt that he was wholly responsible for the sabotage. I let out a breath of relief, as always wondering why I ever doubted my friend—for had he ever let me, or one of his clients, down?

Meanwhile, the humans were still reacting to the shock. "Cecil!" the prince's wife, Princess Alexandra of Denmark, exclaimed loudly. "Naughty cat—did you do that?"

"Unobservant humans," Basil muttered under his breath. "Surely they must realize—"

Before he could finish, one of the prince's siblings, Princess Helena, spoke up. "It wasn't Cecil," she said. "There are claw marks clearly visible on the print. See? And cats retract their claws, while dogs cannot."

At that nearly everyone present turned to stare at Pes, who was sniffing around for crumbs of food on the floor. "Pes!" the human King of Bohemia roared. "That blasted mutt . . ." He went on for some time in his native language, while Prince Leo looked sullen. But the upshot was that Pes was blamed for the crime and banished to Leo's room for the remainder of the visit. What's more, the adult Bohemians insisted that the troublesome dog be confined for the journey home as well—to the great relief of the Bohemian mice.

After that the party continued. With Pes absent, we were able to sneak out to sample the human food—a fine way to celebrate Basil's successful photo sabotage!

Speaking of which, he finally filled us in on the details of how he'd done it, though I confess that I had little understanding of modern photography and didn't retain much of the information. But I understood enough to know that he and Marek—who had much more intimate knowledge of the dimensions of Pes's paws, as well as the location of the young mice in the photo—had somehow smudged out the real images with the fake paw print, finishing only moments before the photographer reached down to grab the plate and begin the development process.

"Genius!" the duke said, giving Basil a hearty slap on the back. "I'm glad I called you in, Basil."

"I am too, Your Grace," Basil said with a slight bow. "It's an honor to be of use to the royal family."

I didn't hear whatever Basil said next, as my attention was caught by the sight of Marek stepping over to join Clara in a quiet corner of the space. He was holding a delectable bit of cake, stolen from the party outside, which he offered to her. But she merely turned away, and I thought I could see tears in her eyes.

"Spying on the youth, Dawson?" Basil said in my ear, startling me.

I jumped and turned with a chuckle. "Perhaps a bit," I admitted. "But I'm concerned, Basil. Why do those two dislike each other so much?" I gestured toward the pair in question.

Basil glanced at them, then smiled. "Ah, Dawson," he said. "Don't you see it? I've had a suspicion all along, of course, but now it's so clear. . . ."

"What?" I was perplexed as to what he was talking about.

Instead of answering, he turned and called for attention. "Please, all of you," he said. "There's something I need to tell you. Something important . . ."

15

AN EVENT TO CELEBRATE

AS THE OTHERS GATHERED AROUND, BASIL FINALLY revealed the secret he'd discovered. "It's Clara and Marek," he said, pointing to the pair, who looked surprised. "Can't you see it? They're in love!"

There were gasps from all around—none louder than that emitted by Clara herself. "How did you know?" she blurted out. She rounded on Marek. "Did you tell him?"

But Marek seemed as shocked as anyone. "No!" he exclaimed. "You made me promise not to breathe a word. And I would never break a promise to you."

Now I saw it! How could I have missed it

before? As Marek gazed longingly at Clara, it all became as plain as the whiskers on my face. They were, indeed, in love!

"We didn't want anyone to know," Marek explained to the group. "What is the point, after all? It can never work out. She lives here in England, and I . . ." He let out a long sigh. "I must soon return to far-off Bohemia."

"What?" Marek's father roared. A huge smile broke out across his face. "Are you a complete fool, my boy? Why should distance be of any concern?"

"Yes," Basil put in. "The human royal families intermarry frequently—just look at the prince himself and his royal wife, who was born in far-off Denmark."

The Queen of Bohemia nodded. "Why should mice be any different?" she said. "This is wonderful news!"

"Yes," the duke added. "And the perfect excuse for many more visits between our families!"

"You must come to Bohemia next," the king insisted, bowing to the duke and duchess. "It will be our honor to host you."

There came many more words after that, but in summary, the parents were delighted, along with the rest of the family. They insisted that Clara and

Marek share the next dance, and the young couple did so, still looking a little stunned—but also blissfully happy.

"And that's another case closed," Basil commented, looking pleased with himself as we watched. And who could blame him? For who else but the world-renowned Basil of Baker Street could play matchmaker, photographer's assistant, and detective all in one day?

Very late that night, Basil and I made our way through a slumbering London toward home. The royals had offered us lodging for the night, but I had patients to see the next day, and Basil was eager to be back in Holmestead as well—probably because Mr. Holmes was due home early the next morning.

"Won't you miss the luxury of Marlborough House, though?" I asked him as we walked, thinking back over the past two days' adventures.

Basil shrugged. "No need to miss it, Dawson," he said, looking sly. "We'll be returning soon enough."

"We will?" I said in surprise. "How so, my friend?"

Basil smiled. "Marek's father, the king, stopped me on my way out just now," he said. "Make sure your best suit is pressed, Dawson—because very soon we'll be attending a royal wedding!"

I was too surprised to answer. But in any case, Basil gave me little opportunity before he spoke again.

"Now, let's shake a paw, Dawson," he said, hurrying forward across a cobbled street. "I want to get a good night's rest before Mr. Holmes returns. I'm looking forward to hearing about his latest escapades."

I had little doubt of that—though I also had little doubt that even the great man's adventures could hold a candle to those of myself and my dear friend Basil of Baker Street!